The Mole and The Violin

Best Wishes

The Mole and The Violin

A Chapter Book for Young Readers

George E. Brummell

Library of Congress Control Number: 2013902570
ISBN: Hardcover 978-1-4797-9333-4
Softcover 978-1-4797-9332-7
Ebook 978-1-4797-9334-1

This book was printed in the United States of America.

Rev. date: 02/14/2013

To order additional copies of this book, contact:
Xlibris Corporation
1-888-795-4274
www.Xlibris.com
Orders@Xlibris.com
128415

"George Brummell, whose artistry has already been demonstrated in his first book, a memoir titled "Shades of Darkness," has done so again in his first book for children, "The Mole and the Violin." As with C.S. Lewis's "Narnian Chronicles," Brummell makes the magical real with his attentiveness and sensitivity to the actual world and that which lies beyond it. We know that humans and other species can communicate with each other and, in this book, as in actual life, music serves as the universal language. My firm belief is that this tender and inspiring book is the beginning of a "song without end." George Brummell understands that which brings all of us together; he understands life and helps us to do so as well. I want him to continue."

Dr. Peter I. Hartsock
Captain, U.S. Public Health Service

Contents

I dedicate this book to all my grandchildren,
especially to Emma and her music and to those
children of Newtown whose futures were taken
while they blossomed with life.
May we always remember.

Acknowledgments

Thanks to Jessica L. Umana for contributing her photo for the image on the book cover and her father Elmer A. Umana for taking the photograph.

Thanks to Alex Umana for his contribution.

Thanks to Heather Petsche, Jodi Pankowski, and Willie Robinson for taking the time to review the manuscript and offering useful suggestions.

Thanks to Dr. Edward Gabriele, Dr. Peter Hartsock, and Elisabeth Friend for their constructive comments and their review of the illustrations.

Thanks to my wife, Maria, for her unwavering support.

Also I want to thank Lorenzo Clark for his help in reviewing the Galley and offering suggestions.

About the Author

George Brummell is the author of his memoir *Shades of Darkness*. He is retired from the US Army, a war veteran blinded as result of a mine explosion in Vietnam. He is also a retired National Field Services director for the Blinded Veterans Association and a graduate of the University of Akron with a degree in social work. Despite his injuries, he is very active—riding his tandem, writing, public speaking, and traveling the world with his wife, Maria.

He lives in Silver Spring, Maryland, and enjoys visiting area schools, motivating children about his journey. While conducting a writing workshop at an area elementary school, he noticed that children responded positively to his unique circumstances, which motivated him to write a book for young readers. Since blindness is a subject he is very familiar, he chose a mole as the protagonist. George felt Mikey the mole was much like him—independent, curious and didn't let sightlessness get in his way.

He got the idea of the instrument from his violin-playing granddaughter, Emma. At a very young age, she inspired him with her hard work, discipline, and persistence to master the instrument. George's positive, upbeat attitude and interesting stories have motivated children in classrooms to better their writing and reading skills. Now he wants to motivate through *The Mole and the Violin*, a book that introduces young readers to a nearly forgotten creature that survives in a dark underground environment and to the beauty of the violin.

I loved the story and appreciate you allowing me to pre-read it. This story is awesome and culturally diverse. It brings an acceptance to blindness, and shyness as well as expressing that no-one can prevent anyone else from dreaming. It has a strong family bond across generations and accepts differences. It also recognizes the arts and how important they are as band, chorus, dance, and strings are always at risk of being removed from school curriculum.

Jodi Pankowski
Principal, Independent Hill and Pace

For the Child in Each of Us

Edward Gabriele
Author, Poet, Teacher

Children are fascinating. Stories written about them or for them are equally so. In the pages to follow, you will enter into an amazing world. George Brummell's work *The Mole and the Violin* will stoke your imagination and fill you with wonder. The tale of Mikey the mole and his friendship with Emma the violinist is more than a story. It is an experience and a journey.

But an experience of what? A journey where?

These questions require a bit of reflection.

We adults treasure our experiences with children and the stories for and about them. Both are precious. We hear our children laugh, and it moves us to laugh with equal energy. We hear them cry or we hear horrific tragedies such as the one that befell the children at Sandy Hook Elementary School, and we are overwhelmed with sadness.

We walk into our children's bedrooms and see them sleeping, and we watch with a tenderness that cannot be captured in simple words. When we encounter little ones in life, we treasure in them all that we have been and wish still to be. In them, we see our own dreams, hopes, fears, loves, joys, our very selves.

In *The Mole and the Violin*, we have an exquisite story where a seemingly insignificant animal from the dark corridors of the earth burrows his way daringly up to the surface. He risks to experience something different. When Mikey unearths himself, he hears something so beautiful that he cannot help but follow its path—even though it means risking a possible encounter with real danger. He risks and runs headlong into a creature making the most beautiful sounds he has ever heard. Suddenly he knows the experience of desire. He wants to be caught up in the beauty of what he hears, and this leads him to befriend the human girl, Emma. She cannot believe he talks. He cannot believe she cares. His search and her amazement bring them together as friends; and suddenly they come to teach each other things utterly new and wondrous.

Like all other children's stories, *The Mole and the Violin* is just as much for adults. The pages you are about to turn are more than just a story. They are the doorway into an experience—an experience of who we are and all we wish to be as humans, as family members, as friends, as citizens of this wonderful planet, as the dreaming children we never cease to be.

George Brummell has given us a gift far greater than just a story. Like all children's literature, he has given us a story that we do not just read to ourselves or to our children. He has given us a living pathway on which we journey with our children toward that moment we all crave when our dreams might become waking realities.

As you burrow through the following pages, listen carefully. You too just might hear the sound of something musically wonderful.

But be careful. It just might make you want to burrow open your heart to a stranger, sing to a melody our world too often does not hear, and learn to love enough to make a new music that sets all the world a'dancing.

Chapter One

"Don't dig too deep, and don't dig far away," Mikey's mother told him as he went off to search for food.

"Oh, mom, don't worry. I'll not get lost!" Mikey shouted back from the tunnel.

Mikey was a mole with soft gray fur and a pink snout. He was larger than most mole boars his age but quite shy. Mikey had four big front teeth, two upper and two lower, which came in handy because, every day, he ate his own weight in food. His hunger kept him very busy searching.

On this fine autumn day, he was digging in the dark through wet soil, hunting for worms. Like all moles, Mikey was nearly blind, although vision doesn't help much in the dark underground. The sensitive hairs on his nose and front legs told him all he needed to know to get around. Believe it or not, Mikey could catch and eat a worm in one second!

Because he was an adventurous mole, he stretched the rule about digging far from home. He wanted to see how far he could dig in one day, and this day, his digging brought him to a new place—very damp and full of interesting roots. He was squeezing a worm between his paws to clean off the dirt when he heard a strange, beautiful sound.

He tipped his head up; the sound had come from just above him. *What's that?* he wondered, as the worm wiggled free of his paws.

Mikey's excellent hearing helped make up for his lack of vision. He listened closely to the lovely sound, trying to understand what it might be, but nothing he had ever heard sounded like this.

To hear better, he scraped his way up toward the sound until he broke through to the surface. He breathed in the cool, fresh air and listened.

What he was hearing, though he didn't know it, was music. The melody made him very happy. In the daylight, Mikey could see shapes: a tree and a house. Nearby, just a few feet away, something tall was moving fast and slow and fast again. He could tell that the sound was coming from this odd figure.

Forgetting that the surface was a place of danger, he moved closer to the music. Now he could see the shadowy shape of something tall constantly moving under a tree. He knew that the sound wouldn't hurt him. How could danger come from such a beautiful sound?

Mikey hid in the grass and listened. The music made him joyous and calm at the same time. Later, he would learn that it had a name—the Violin Concerto in D Major—and that a man named Tchaikovsky had composed it.

For now, though, he only knew that the wonderful sound made him feel very peaceful—so peaceful that, before long, he fell asleep.

Chapter Two

When Mikey woke up, the music and the music maker were gone. Finding himself in daylight, he panicked. He had broken Mole Rule Number One: "Never sleep above ground." Lucky for him, no cat or hawk or skunk had seen him in the grass.

His older friends, Frankie and Sammy, had also listened to the music. Hearing their voices, he dug down toward them. As soon as he broke through the tunnel wall, he shouted excitedly, "Did you hear what I heard? I want to learn how to do that!"

Frankie laughed at him. "Are you crazy? That's a girl, a human, playing a violin. Moles don't play violins!"

Sammy joined in the teasing. "I always knew you were weird," he said, "but I didn't think you were *that* weird!"

"If this is a joke," Frankie said, "it's a good one!"

Mikey's spirit was bruised but not broken. Even though his friends had laughed at him, they couldn't stop him from dreaming. He dug his way back toward home, alone.

"Mommy!" he shouted as he entered the chamber. "Guess what! I heard something amazing above the ground—Sammy and Frankie said it was a human playing a violin!"

Even though he tried to hide it, Mother Mole sensed that something was wrong. Behind his excitement, she could hear that he was upset. Placing a paw on his shoulder, she asked if he was sad.

He said, "Only because they told me I can't learn to play a violin. But I don't believe them!"

Mother Mole rubbed Mikey's back to comfort him and explained things as gently as she could. "I'm sorry, Mikey, but violins are for people, not moles. You can't play a violin in a mole tunnel—it just wouldn't fit. And you certainly can't play it above ground, where some old snake could get you."

"But I want to learn! I *have* to learn!"

"No, Mikey, I'm sorry, but there's no future for a mole playing a violin. That's not the kind of work moles do."

"What kind of work do moles do?" he asked.

"Well—usually something to do with digging. You know your father is a construction worker."

"I don't want to do that," Mikey said. "I want to play a violin. At least I want to try!"

Mother Mole sighed and went back to sweeping the chamber. She knew she wouldn't be able to talk Mikey out of his new interest, but she hoped he would forget it in a day or two.

That night, Mikey dreamed that he was one of the world's greatest violinists. Even though he didn't know exactly what a violin looked like, he saw himself moving his arms and making beautiful music, just like the little girl did.

In the morning, he decided to go find her again and ask her to teach him how to play.

Chapter Three

As Mikey dug, he stopped only to eat the juiciest centipedes and grubs. Soon he reached the tunnel he had dug the day before. To his joy, he heard a new melody, even more pleasing to his ears than yesterday's. It was the girl again, singing as she played.

Mikey dug closer and closer to the sound until he broke through a little molehill right at the little girl's feet. She stopped playing and singing and bent down to look at Mikey.

He blinked a couple of times to clear the soil from his eyes. Though he couldn't see clearly, he saw that she only had fur on her head. It was long, black, and curly. Her face and arms and legs were smooth and a lighter color. The parts in between seemed to be covered with bright colors. She had a sweet, clean smell.

The young girl had seen pictures of moles in a book. She said, "Hello, little mole," never expecting the animal to answer her.

"Hello," Mikey said, in the tiniest little voice.

A hole seemed to open in her face. It was her mouth, he realized.

"Did you just say *hello*?" she asked.

"Yes, I did."

She placed the violin in its case and dropped down on her knees. Her face came closer. "You can talk?"

"Of course," Mikey said. "But I can't play the violin, and I want to learn."

The girl could scarcely believe what she was hearing.

"By the way," the mole said, "my name is Mikey. What's yours?"

"My name is Emma, and I am very happy to meet you."

"Do you know," Mikey said, "I think you must be a genius because you make such beautiful music."

Emma liked Mikey more and more with every word he said. As it happened, Mikey was correct: Emma *was* a genius. She had played the violin since she was two years old. Her grandfather, a violinist and a violin maker, had made her a special instrument just her size, and he built a new one each year. Although she was only nine, she had already performed in concert halls in six cities.

"What were you playing just now?" Mikey asked. "It was so wonderful."

"That was Mozart's *Ave Maria*. Thank you very much."

"Do you think you could teach me to play it?"

Emma couldn't help herself; she laughed. Mikey's feelings were hurt. She could tell by the way he hung his head.

"I'm sorry, it's just that I've never met a talking mole before, and now I've met one who wants to learn to play the violin!"

"I know it's unusual," Mikey said. "But I'm sure I can do it!"

She studied his tiny body and couldn't imagine how he could even hold a violin and bow, let alone play. But she didn't want to hurt his feelings again.

"I'm not sure, Mikey," she said. "Your legs are kind of bent. And short."

"Maybe I can find a violin small enough to fit me. We moles are very determined."

Emma knew that moles lived in the dark and that they learned about the world mainly through hearing and touch. *I wonder*, she thought, *if Granddad could make him a tiny violin* . . .

But how could she explain why she needed it? If she told him it was for a talking mole—

"Kena!" she shouted suddenly, happily.

Mikey had no idea what that word meant, but Emma soon explained. "Kena is my favorite doll. I can tell Granddad I want a violin for Kena! She's just a little bigger than you!"

Mikey was so excited, he clapped his little pink paws together. "Will you teach me?" he asked Emma.

"I can try," she said. "Who knows? No one believed I could learn to play when I was two, but I did."

She told Mikey to come back at the same time in three days—but then she wondered how he would know when it was the right time. "Can you tell time?" she asked.

"Sure can," he answered quickly.

"But how?"

"My Dad made a tunnel to the surface so we could always check the weather. I can tell the time from where the sun is in the sky."

Wow, Emma thought. *This is not an average family of moles*.

Chapter Four

Back in her room, Emma took Kena from the shelf above her bed and studied her closely. The size seemed just about right.

She phoned her grandfather and said, "Granddad, do you think you could make me a tiny violin?"

Emma's Granddad, George, would do anything for his only grandchild, but he always pretended to be sterner than he really was. "Now why in the world could you possibly want a tiny violin, young lady?"

"It's for one of my dolls," she said. "I know it sounds silly, but I want Kena to have a violin just like mine. Could you come over so I can show you?"

Her grandfather lived across the street and a few houses down. Emma watched from her window as he locked his door and came strolling happily toward her home.

"My hero!" she said and gave him a hug that warmed him all the way to his bones. He really was a hero who had won many medals in a long-ago war, but her love meant more to him than all the medals in the world.

"Now which of your little friends needs a violin?" he asked with a smile.

She led him by the hand to her dresser where she had placed Kena: a very beautiful doll, about six inches tall, with huge eyes, brown skin, and thick black curls down to her knees. Kena had on jeans and a T-shirt. It was hard to imagine her playing the violin.

"I want to change her into a classical musician like me," Emma said. "I'm going to get her a black gown and teach her how to play."

"Are you telling me this has to be an actual, working violin?"

"Of course! What good would it be if it didn't work?"

Her grandfather laughed. "All I can say is, I hope your friend learns as quickly as you did. I wouldn't want my hard work to go to waste."

"I promise it won't!" Emma said and gave her Granddad a happy kiss on the cheek.

Three days later, Emma watched Mikey pop up from the ground in the same place where they had first met. This time, she had her doll, Kena, with her.

"Sorry I'm late," Mikey said. "I found some worms and grubs on the way. They were so tasty, I forgot about the time."

"Let me see something, Mikey. Stand up, please."

He stood up as best he could on the grass. She placed Kena beside him. The doll was a good two inches taller than Mikey. She hoped the little violin her grandfather was making would fit and regretted not measuring more carefully.

"Do you have my violin?" he asked.

"Not yet. My Granddad says it'll take another week—that's seven more sunrises."

Even on that tiny mole face, Emma could see Mikey's disappointment.

"But guess what? I brought my violin so I could give you your first lesson today. Are you ready to start learning?"

"Yes!"

"Come very close."

She lay down on the grass and placed the violin under her chin so that he could put his face right up to the strings.

"These are strings. There are four of them. Each one makes a different note, and we call the notes G, D, A, and E."

She plucked each string because she couldn't use the bow in that awkward position.

"Now you try. Reach up with a claw, and pluck one string at a time."

Mikey was so excited, his little paw trembled. When he heard the deep sound of the G string made by his own claw, he quivered with the greatest joy he had ever felt.

"Now here," she said, "is a pitch pipe. If you blow into it, it will make the same notes as the strings. That's so you can tune the strings."

"What does that mean?"

She realized how little moles know about violins and sighed.

"Well, sometimes—a *lot* of the time—the strings get a bit loose, and you have to tighten them, or they make the wrong sounds."

She blew into each of the pitch pipe's four tubes and turned the pegs one at a time so that the strings made the exact same notes as the pitch pipe.

Mikey got very excited. "Can I try?" he asked.

Emma thought about that. "You know," she said, "I think I'm going to give you a pitch pipe of your own to blow into. I don't want you to catch any of my germs."

"That's very considerate of you," Mikey said.

"Now, the way you make a sound on a violin is very special," Emma explained. "And very hard to do well! You take your bow"—she sat up so she could demonstrate—"and you pull it straight across the strings very lightly. Like this."

As she drew her bow across the E string, Mikey shivered. To him, it sounded like the sweetest, gentlest voice that ever sang a song. "That's the sound! That's the sound I want to make!"

"You will, Mikey, you will. As soon as Granddad finishes your violin, I'll teach you. But you have to be patient. It takes a while to learn how to make that sound."

"I'll be patient! I promise!"

"Good. I'll see you in exactly one week."

"I can't wait a whole week!"

She laughed. "You promised to be patient!"

"Oh. Right. I can hardly wait—but I will!"

Chapter Five

When she saw the tiny violin in her grandfather's palm, Emma was so excited that she leaped straight up in the air. The violin was made of pale oak wood, with a bow the size of a bobby pin. She pinched the tiny bow between her fingertips and drew it across the strings. The tone was lovely and sweet, like a mouse softly singing.

"Mikey will love it!" she said. "I mean, Kena will."

"I'm really looking forward to your first duet," Granddad said, laughing.

"You know what?" Emma said. "We may surprise you."

Her grandfather kept chuckling. "You sure will, if your doll plays this violin."

"Mikey! Mikey! Wake up!"

She had arrived early at their meeting place, but he'd gotten there even earlier and fallen asleep. He jumped at the sound of her voice and dived back into his hole, afraid for his life. But when he peeked out again, he smelled her sweet shampoo and remembered why he was there.

"Look what I have for you," she said and held the violin up close to his face.

At first, he couldn't make out much, just a general shape. As he squinted, he realized it must be his violin because its strings were glinting in the sun, just like Emma's.

It was a bright, hot afternoon. Mikey would always remember the blue sky behind his violin because it was the most beautiful sight he had ever seen.

"Let's see if it's the right size," Emma said.

Standing on his rear legs, he stretched out his front paws. Emma placed the violin in them and showed him how to tuck the chin rest between his chin and chest while holding the neck with his left paw. Then she gave him the bow.

"May I try?"

"Please do!"

He pulled the bow across the strings the way she had shown him. A scratchy whistling noise came from the violin.

It was all Mikey could do to keep from crying. He didn't want to hurt Emma's feelings, but her grandfather had obviously made a very bad violin.

"Don't worry," she said, "that's how everyone sounds the first time they try. It can take *years* before you learn to make a beautiful sound. That's what I meant about being patient."

"Are you sure" . . ." He hesitated to say it. "Are you sure this violin really *can* make a nice sound?"

She took it from him and pulled the bow across the strings with an expert touch. Again, it sang. Mikey turned a somersault and rolled in the grass. "It works!" he said. "My violin works!"

Next, Emma taught him some of the important basics: tightening the bow to make a space between the hairs and the wood, how to hold the bow, where the bow should contact the string, how hard to press down with the bow and how quickly to move it, and what to do when you reach the end of the bow. (Push it back the other way!)

Mikey watched and listened closely, squinting the whole time, doing exactly what Emma did.

Even though he tried his hardest, he still made a scratchy sound. This was impossible! It was like telling him to jump over a tree; no matter how much he practiced, he would never be able to do it.

Emma saw what she thought might be tears in Mikey's eyes. To encourage him, she said, "Wow, you sound much better than I did the first time I tried. You must be a very fast learner."

That changed everything. Mikey's spirits rose from discouragement to hopefulness again. He thought, *I won't be an ordinary mole anymore, just digging in the dirt all day. I'm going to be a* violinist*!*

"Now all you have to do is keep practicing," Emma said. "Just keep at it every day. Little by little, you'll start to sound even better."

"I can't wait!"

She laughed. "You *have* to wait! Remember? Be patient."

Mikey laughed along with her. He had rarely been so happy.

CHAPTER SIX

The first time Mikey practiced, it caused quite a stir underground. All the moles in the neighborhood poked their noses out into the main tunnel, confused and upset. "What's that awful noise?" old Mrs. Grubdinger asked. "It's horrible!"

Mikey's mother agreed. "It just doesn't make sense," she said. "You're wasting your time. And you're hurting everyone's ears."

Frankie and Sammy came scampering into Mikey's chamber and laughed their heads off when they found him on his hind legs, playing the violin. "That's the most ridiculous thing I ever saw!" Frankie said.

"It sounds so bad, it should be against the law," Sammy added.

"How long are you going to keep making that terrible sound?" Frankie asked.

"Until I get it right," Mikey told him and kept playing.

At Mikey's next lesson, Emma thought she could hear a real improvement, and she told him so. When she tried to teach him about holding the strings down to make different notes, though, they found a problem: his claws. She kept her own nails short so they didn't get in the way of playing. She asked if he would like her to clip his claws. He said, horrified, "No! How would I dig?"

It took some struggle, but Mikey learned to hold down the strings in spite of his claws. That proved to Emma that this little mole had true determination. His intelligence and discipline amazed her.

Back in his dark chamber, Mikey experimented with his violin, putting different amounts of pressure on the bow, always trying to get a better sound. To the dismay of his neighbors, he practiced for hours, struggling to unlock the mystery. His mother kept hoping he would give up and go back to his normal mole life, but that didn't happen.

One day, after more than a month of practice, something changed. The scratchy, terrible noise softened. Suddenly, the tune Emma had shown him—Brahms's Lullaby—sounded like music. Without ever noticing it, his little paws had found the secret.

Mrs. Grubdinger lifted her head up and thought, *That's not so bad after all.*

Mikey's Mom thought the exact same thing.

And Frankie and Sammy went right past Mikey's chamber without teasing him.

Emma taught him other songs—some classical, some popular, some slow, some fast. When she taught him her father's favorite song, "Dancing in the Street," it caused a big sensation in Mikey's community. His mother, who had never danced before, started swaying in time with the music. She didn't know what she was doing, but she couldn't help herself. It felt good! "You sound better, Mikey!" she called out.

Every living creature nearby started moving. Worms poked their heads out of his chamber's walls to hear and wiggled to the music. Music was new to the underground creatures.

Although Mikey had a lot of discipline, it was hard to stay focused on music when he could hear the worms wiggling nearby. But he knew that by the time he set down the violin and bow and pounced, the worms would disappear—he knew because he had tried to catch them more than once!—so he kept playing even when he heard temptation wiggling nearby.

Chapter Seven

By this time, the weather had turned cold again. Emma told Mikey that she wouldn't be able to give him more lessons until spring because it was too cold for a human to stay outside. From the way he hung his head, she saw how disappointed he was. "Will you hibernate?" she asked, hoping that maybe the winter would pass quickly for him.

"No, we don't do that. We get too hungry."

"Well . . . I'll come out now and then and listen for you. Keep practicing!"

He took that encouragement as a command. All that winter, he kept playing the songs she had taught him and even made up a few melodies of his own, just for fun. Some of them were based on the sounds of his underground world: "Growing Roots," he called one; another was "The Wiggly Worm Dance." (That one scored a big hit with all the invertebrates.) Thanks to his music, every creature living underground had a new pleasure to enjoy beyond eating and sleeping.

He couldn't wait for spring, when he would play for Emma again and see if he had improved as much as he thought.

Just as she had promised, Emma wandered out to their meeting place every now and then, crouched down low, and listened for the sound of Mikey's violin. She never managed to hear it, though. She worried that something might have happened to him or to the violin. Most of all, she worried that he might freeze to death during this long, cold winter.

On the first warm afternoon in March, she brought her violin outside and found Mikey there waiting for her, practicing "In the Hall of the Mountain King" by Grieg. Her mouth dropped open. His playing was so lively, so skillful! But then she thought, *Why should I be surprised by anything a talking mole does?*

"Mikey, you're ready to perform! You should give a concert!"

Never in his life had Mikey's little mole heart swelled with such pride. Praise from Emma meant more than all the worms and grubs in the world.

But there was a problem, Emma realized. What concert hall would allow a mole to perform on its stage? And how would the audience even see Mikey?

She didn't want to disappoint him so soon after getting his hopes up. She said, "Before you can perform, you need to see a great violinist give a concert. That way, you'll know exactly what to do."

"But I've already heard you," he said.

She laughed. "I'm just a student. Wait till you hear a professional!"

By the time she returned to her house, she had a plan. Her grandfather had promised to take her to a concert that weekend. She would take one of her older dolls and remove some of its stuffing. Then she would let Mikey climb inside. With her doll in her lap, Mikey would hear everything. If she held the doll up next to her face now and then, he could even peek out and see the stage. He might not be able to make out many of the details, but she felt sure the experience would mean a lot to him.

Without waiting a moment, she took down her oldest doll. First she took off Susie's long blue evening gown, then she carefully made an opening in front and took out some of the cotton. *Mikey is going to have the time of his life*, she thought.

The next day, though, when she told him her plan, he seemed to shrink up. "I couldn't do that," he said. "I couldn't go so far away from home. Something might eat me."

"Believe me, Mikey, nothing will eat you if you're inside my doll. I'll take very good care of you."

"But it's so scary!"

"I'll never let you out of my hands. I promise."

"But . . . what's a doll?"

She laughed so hard, it hurt his ears. When she held Susie up close to his eyes, all he could see was the shape of a person, like Emma but much smaller.

"Hello," he said.

"Mikey, dolls aren't alive. They're toys!"

Now he was the one who couldn't stop laughing.

"Are you scared, Mikey?" Emma asked in a whisper.

Inside Susie's belly, Mikey felt his heart going as fast as a woodpecker drumming on a branch. Peeking out, he saw blurry shapes going by at a speed he had never dreamed possible. The wind going by outside the convertible sounded like a roar to him. He said, "I'm scared, but I trust you."

"That's good!" she said.

Her grandfather was driving and listening to a symphony on the radio. He said, "Are you having a conversation with your little friend back there?"

"Yes, I am."

"Remember, no talking to your doll during the concert," he said, chuckling.

"Of course not, Granddad."

Chapter Eight

Emma held the doll as if it were a baby cradled in her arms. Mikey knew she would take good care of him, but even so, the bouncing as she walked was so unfamiliar that he grew afraid again. The ground was so far below him, and it was pale gray instead of green. He pulled his head inside Susie's belly so he wouldn't see anything at all.

It was fairly comfortable inside the doll—nice and dark, just like home. As they walked from the car to the concert hall, he kept smelling aromas that he couldn't name but which made him hungry.

"Emma?" he said.

She didn't hear him, so he had to shout it.

Holding the doll's belly up to her ear, she said, "Yes?"

"Do you think you could give me a worm to eat? I'm kind of hungry."

She hadn't thought about that. "Can you eat raisins? I have some in my pocket."

"I don't know. Could I try one?"

Holding Susie close with one arm, she reached for the little red box in her pocket and took out a single raisin. "If you like it, you can have more."

Mikey sniffed the raisin and turned it around with his paws before tasting it. The raisin was unlike any worm or grub he had ever eaten, but he liked the taste. He didn't want to risk getting sick from this strange human food, though. "Could I have just a couple more?"

Emma handed him three more raisins. "If you're still hungry after the concert, Granddad always takes me to Buster's Burgers, and I'll share my food with you."

"Um . . . okay, thanks," Mikey said, though he had no idea what a Buster's Burger might be.

While he was happily chewing on his raisins, a terrifying noise startled him. A ferocious animal ten times his size was barking loudly. He pulled back inside Susie's belly but peeked down just a little and saw a white creature with curly fur, almost as tall as Emma's knee, jumping toward him. Fortunately, a rope around its neck kept it from getting too close.

"I'm so sorry," the woman holding the rope said. "I don't know what's come over Pierre."

Emma hid behind Granddad, protecting Mikey. "I don't think he likes dolls," Granddad said, laughing.

The creature named Pierre had sharp white teeth, each one as long as Mikey's whole paw, and he showed them as he growled.

"Shame on you, Pierre! It's just a doll!"

Emma held Susie so close that Mikey could feel her heart beating. Although he had never been so frightened in his life, he had to admit it felt nice to be held so snugly in her arms.

From Susie's belly, Mikey watched Emma's grandfather hand something small and white to a woman in uniform. Then they started climbing stairs. He couldn't see the steps very well, but they seemed to be red. Finally, they reached their seats, and Emma put Susie in her lap. "I hope you enjoy this, Susie," she said.

"I hope so, too," Granddad said. "We're lucky they don't charge extra for dolls."

The lights went dim. Mikey liked that because it felt more like home. Suddenly, he heard a loud, exciting crash; he didn't know it then, but he was hearing cymbals. He couldn't even imagine what sort of instrument would make such a sound, and he wanted to ask Emma but didn't want to bother her.

When the rest of the orchestra joined in, Mikey was overjoyed. The best sounds he had ever produced on the violin were just noise compared with this. The music was so beautiful, he started swaying inside Susie. That made Emma laugh, which made her Granddad shush her.

Later in the concert, something terrible and embarrassing happened to Mikey. He had to do something, and he knew he must not do it inside the doll—but how could he explain this to Emma? What was even worse, he needed to do it very soon, and the music was so loud that she couldn't hear him calling her name.

Finally, he had to beat his paws against the doll's back with all his strength so she would feel it. "Ssh, you're tickling me," she whispered.

He didn't stop because it was an emergency. As soon as she lifted the doll to her ear, he called to her, "Got to get out. Got to go—got to go—can't wait!"

She understood. "Granddad," she whispered in his ear, "Susie needs the bathroom."

"Susie *what*? Are you kidding?" But then he realized what she meant. "I see. I guess nature calls for dolls too."

And he led Emma and Susie past some annoyed music lovers to the aisle.

Chapter Nine

Luckily, there wasn't anyone in the ladies' room. Emma placed Mikey on the rim of the seat and closed the door to give him privacy.

A moment later, she heard a splash.

She had no choice but to fish him out. Immediately, she carried him over to the sink and gave him a bath.

"Emma, what are you doing to me?" Mikey asked, in a panic. "My fur is all white!"

"It's called a bath," she explained, "and that's soap. "You'll be the cleanest mole in history."

At first he didn't like getting all wet, but the soap smelled nice, and the water was much warmer than rain, and he decided that he liked his bath very much—at least, until she tried to dry him with a paper towel. "Hey, stop that!" he shouted.

"But we have to dry you off."

"No, you don't. It's okay for me to be wet. It keeps my skin moist."

She was just about to put Mikey back inside Susie when an elderly woman came into the room. This woman had very thick glasses, and she greeted Emma in a friendly way. "Are you enjoying the concert?" she asked.

Emma jumped in front of Mikey, hiding him. "Oh, yes. Very much."

"Well, you'd better get back to your seat before you miss the last piece."

"Yes, you're right" . . .

She reached behind her. Mikey hopped onto her hand, and she closed her fingers gently around him.

When she came out of the ladies' room, Granddad said, a bit impatiently, "I never knew dolls took so long to do their business."

As she had promised, Emma talked Granddad into a stop at Buster's Burgers after the concert.

With Susie sitting in the corner of the booth, below the level of the table, it was easy for Emma to slip little bits of hamburger to Mikey without Granddad noticing. At first he squeezed the meat to clean the dirt off, but he found that, as hard as he worked, the darkness wouldn't come off. Since he was too hungry to wait, he ate the bit of meat just as it was.

He had never eaten anything as delicious as this and didn't think he ever would until she gave him half of what she called a French fry. Wow!

"This is great!" he whispered, and she giggled.

After Buster's, Granddad wanted to visit his sister, Emma's Great-Aunt Mary, who lived just a couple blocks away. Mary was one of Emma's favorite relatives, but Emma was a bit worried about Mikey. It might not be healthy for him to stay above ground for so long. She realized that she didn't know much about moles and their needs.

"I hope we don't stay too long," she told her Granddad. "I'm starting to feel kind of tired."

"Don't you worry, we'll just say a quick hello. You know how happy it makes her to see you."

Mikey was very glad they wouldn't be staying long because, even though he was enjoying the adventure, he missed his home and his freedom.

Emma's Great-Aunt Mary gave her such a big hug that she had to hold Susie off to the side to protect Mikey from getting crushed. The three of them sat together at Mary's kitchen table, talking, until finally Emma said, "Granddad, do you think you could hold Susie for a minute? I have to go."

"But you—" Granddad seemed puzzled that she would need the bathroom again so soon, but he shook his head and laughed. "Sure thing, Emma. I'll hold her."

Granddad didn't realize how important his promise was, though. He set Susie down on the kitchen table and joined his sister on the living room couch as soon as Emma left the room.

Inside Susie, Mikey closed his eyes and remembered the beautiful music he had heard. He'd had so many firsts today: his first concert, first bath, first hamburger, and first French fry. *It really pays to be brave and try new things*, he thought.

Then he heard something he had never heard before. It was a strange chattering noise. When he peeked out of the slit in Susie's dress, he saw a calico cat's green eyes, close enough for him to see almost clearly. The cat's jaws were twitching.

Although he had never seen a cat up close before, something inside him made him freeze. The cat was sniffing the doll all over. Mikey trembled—the cat jumped back and watched the doll suspiciously. Then it came closer again and pushed the doll with its nose, off the table and onto the floor. As if the fall weren't bad enough, the cat sank its sharp teeth into Susie's arm and dragged the doll off into a dark little room.

More terrified than he had ever been in his life, Mikey burrowed deep into Susie's stuffing. The cat was digging with its claws now, trying to reach the meal it knew lay hidden inside. Mikey begged Emma with his thoughts to come save him. There wasn't anything else he could do.

The point of a tooth poked him in the paw, but he pulled away in time. He shouted, "Help! Emma! Help!"

At the same instant, he heard Emma shouting, "Where's Susie? Granddad, where's Susie?"

"I left her on the kitchen table."

"She's not there!"

"Uh-oh," Mary said. "Hercules! Where are you, you naughty cat?"

Mikey heard Emma's little feet running all over the house. Mary's heavier feet moved more slowly, while Granddad's, with the extra thump of a cane, moved slowest of all. Still, he was the one who rescued Mikey.

"Aha! What's this? You're keeping a killer cat, Sis."

He bent with a groan and picked Susie up off the floor. More painful than the fall or the cat's tooth was Granddad cleaning Susie off before returning her to Emma.

"I'm sorry, Sweetheart. I never thought a cat would go after a doll."

Emma grabbed Susie from her grandfather and held her close as she ran out of the room.

"Mikey, are you all right?" she whispered. "Are you hurt?"

"I'm okay. But I'd really like to go home now. Could I go home?"

"Yes, I'll ask Granddad right now."

Mikey fell asleep in the car. He dreamed that he was underground and had stumbled on a chamber full of wiggling worms. It was a very happy dream.

Chapter Ten

When he awoke, he was in darkness. Emma had promised to take him home, but she was tired and decided to take a nap. Mikey was still inside Susie—and there was Emma, fast asleep on her bed, right next to him. He waited awhile then made his way out of Susie and tried to wake her.

"Emma! Wake up! You said you would take me home!"

It was no use. Even poking her arm didn't wake her.

He couldn't wait until morning. His mother would be worried sick about him. He had to go home, and he had to leave right now.

It was a long way down to the floor, but Emma had a knitted bedspread, and Mikey climbed down it like a ladder, putting his claws into the stitches. It was the first time he had ever climbed backward, and his claws got stuck a couple times, but eventually he made it to the carpet. *What a relief to be on the ground again!* he thought.

He went from room to room, searching for a way out of the house in the darkness, but couldn't find an open door. His search went on for so long that he started to panic.

The strange smell of cheese distracted him. Following his nose, he came upon a small lump of cheddar cheese sitting on top of a neat piece of wood. Just as he was about to climb up onto the little wooden platform, he heard a squeaky voice cry out, "Stop!"

He stopped, afraid. *This cheese must be private property*, he thought. He hoped whoever owned it wouldn't be too mad at him.

"Get away from there!" the cheese owner commanded him.

He backed away from the cheese sadly. "I'm sorry," he said. "I didn't know it was yours."

Whoever had called to him thought that was funny. "It's not mine," the voice laughed. "It's a trap!"

Peering around, squinting, he couldn't see who was speaking until a little gray mouse approached. The two sniffed at each other curiously.

"What *are* you?" the mouse asked him.

"I'm a mole. What are you?"

"I'm a mouse, of course. My name is Shalonda. How come I've never seen you before?"

"Well, I live outside. I've never been in Emma's house before. Could you help me find a way out?"

"Gladly. I was afraid we'd have to share our food with you, and there's hardly enough for my family as it is."

Because of Mikey's poor vision, he never thought much about whether other creatures *looked* attractive. All he noticed was if they smelled good or made beautiful sounds. But something about Shalonda struck him as . . . cute. She had delicate pink paws and big black eyes and pretty round ears.

"Thanks for saving me from the trap," he said. "I really wouldn't want to end up in some kind of cage."

Shalonda laughed. "Oh, you wouldn't have ended up in a cage," she said. "It's much worse than that."

As Shalonda led the way, she pointed out her favorite places in the house, including the narrow space behind the kitchen wall where she and her family lived. "Here's where I sleep. I made a nice bed for myself from their old newspapers. Humans throw so much good stuff away."

Mikey couldn't help himself—he sneezed because this place was full of dust. Not at all his idea of a cozy home.

"Ssh!" Shalonda said. "You'll wake the cat!"

Suddenly, Mikey felt sick. Another cat!

"Are you okay?" Shalonda asked.

"I'm just kind of afraid of cats," he admitted. "Could we go outside now?"

"You're right to be scared of Attila. He'd tear a guy like you to pieces!"

Mikey let out a little moan, and that made Shalonda laugh.

"Don't worry, I'll get you outside," she said.

Before they could leave, though, a few of Shalonda's brothers and sisters came back to the place behind the wall, and they couldn't stop staring at Mikey and asking him questions. "Where do you come from?" "How come you look so weird?" "How did your paws get so big and strong?" "Do you kill things with those claws?"

The one thing they couldn't believe was that he lived underground. "What do you eat—dirt?" a little brother mouse asked.

"No, mostly worms and grubs."

Shalonda finally put an end to all the questions and answers because she was starting to worry that Attila might wake up. Mikey said good-bye to all the mice, and they set off very quickly across the kitchen floor.

The sound of Mikey's claws on the hard tiles was very loud. "Can't you tiptoe or something?" Shalonda whispered, but he had no idea what that meant.

When they were almost at the doorway, a different sound of claws on tiles frightened them both—much bigger claws, belonging to a fat white cat running toward them!

"Run, Mikey, run!"

They rushed out of the kitchen and around the corner. Mikey had a hard time keeping up with the speedy little mouse. The cat tried to turn and follow them, but he went sliding the wrong way, straight out the kitchen, with his claws scraping the floor.

"Here, Mikey—through this hole!"

Mikey ran as fast as he could to a tiny opening where the front door met the doorframe. A moment later, he and Shalonda were outside on the porch, watching Attila's white paw reach out through the hole.

Chapter Eleven

"That was close!" Shalonda said.

"Thanks for getting me out of there," Mikey said. "You saved my life!"

"Don't worry, it was nothing."

Even though Shalonda tried to sound brave, Mikey could hear her panting hard—just like he was panting—and he knew she wasn't just out of breath from running.

In the cool night air, they could hear chirping crickets and a dog barking a few houses away.

"Well, I guess I'll go home now. Thanks again. It was very nice to meet you."

Shalonda didn't answer him. He couldn't see her face very well, and at first, Mikey worried that she didn't like him since she didn't say, "It was nice to meet you, too." But then she said, "Ummmm" . . .

"Is something wrong?"

"I'm just a little afraid," she said. She pointed at Attila's paw, which was still sticking out the door.

"Is there another way back inside?"

"I don't know. I've never been out here before."

Squinting as hard as he could, Mikey looked for Emma's tree, the one he always found her practicing under. That was his landmark—once he spotted it, he knew he could find his way home. He saw some lights and some other houses but didn't see a round tree standing by itself in the grass.

"Maybe we can look all around the house for another entrance," Mikey said. "And you can help me find the tree I'm looking for."

Getting down the steps wasn't fun. Mikey had to hold on to each brick step with his front paws and then let go and drop down to the next step—three times, once for each step. He tried to catch Shalonda as she dropped so she wouldn't get hurt, and they kept tumbling over each other.

"Ouch! Mikey, those claws are so long!"

"Sorry."

They didn't find another way back inside. But Mikey did find the tree in the backyard, and his heart leaped with happiness. Then he had a brilliant idea.

"How would you like to come with me for the night and meet my family?"

"Underground? In the dirt?"

He couldn't see her face in the dark, but he could imagine her wrinkling her nose.

Unfortunately for Shalonda, it was either go underground or stay out here with the barking dogs all night. She decided to go with Mikey.

Mosquitoes buzzed all around them. "So this is grass," Shalonda said. "It feels funny under my paws."

She liked the way the flowers smelled, though. While she paused to sniff at an Easter lily, a loud *skritch* startled her. Next thing she knew, Mikey was chatting with a big grasshopper.

"I'm looking for my tunnel," Mikey said. "I know it's around here somewhere. Have you seen a small hole in the dirt?"

"You moles are always digging, digging, digging," the grasshopper said. "I'm surprised the whole lawn doesn't just fall down, with all those tunnels under us."

"Okay, okay, but is there a hole around here? It should be about this far from the tree."

"You mean this one?"

The grasshopper leaped into the sky. Mikey hurried over to where he landed, and there it was—his hole!

"Shalonda, we're home! Thanks, Mister!"

"Don't mention it."

Mikey happily led the way down into the ground. Shalonda followed, much less happily. "Mikey, it's so dark down here. I can't even see you!"

"I'll keep talking to you—just stay close and follow my voice."

Mikey chattered away, cheerful now that he was back on familiar ground—or under it. Shalonda tried not to be afraid, but she really didn't enjoy the feeling of dirt under her paws or the dampness or the chill. A few times, Mikey turned down a side tunnel, and she tried to follow but ended up bumping her nose against a wall of earth. "Mikey!" she called to him. "Please slow down!"

At last they arrived at the chamber, where Mikey's mother was nervously sweeping the floor with her paws. "My little mole!" she cried as soon as he heard and smelled him. She hugged him tight. "Where have you been? No one could find you! Didn't I tell you never to go exploring far away? What—"

She interrupted herself and started sniffing.

"Who's that with you? Or *what's* that?"

She sounded afraid.

"Don't worry, Mama—that's my friend Shalonda. She's a mouse. She saved my life."

At first, Mikey's mother was very suspicious, having an animal of an entirely different species in her home. "What do you mean, your *friend*?" she asked. "Couldn't you find a mole to be your friend?" But once Mikey told the story of how Shalonda had helped him escape from Emma's house, Mother Mole insisted on giving the little gray mouse a hug.

Although Shalonda politely complimented Mikey's home, the truth was that she couldn't see a thing and was afraid that the ceiling would cave in. When Mikey brought out his violin, however, and started playing the theme from *Swan Lake*, she forgot about where she was and closed her eyes. She knew this song because Emma practiced it often—but it was thrilling to hear her own friend play it!

To Mikey's surprise, Shalonda started singing along. At first, her voice came out as a squeak, but once she warmed up, she sang in a pretty, delicate soprano. The sound was so lovely that Mikey had a hard time concentrating on his own playing—he just wanted to listen.

One by one, all the members of Mikey's family, as well as a few uninvited worms, entered the chamber to hear the concert. There was something both sweet and sad about this song. It cast a melancholy spell over all the moles and sent delicious pangs into their hearts. Moles who had been tunneling nearby stopped to listen. Up on the surface, a grumpy old snake heard the sound and poked his head underground to hear better. Mikey's friend Sammy scrambled away in terror, but the old snake wasn't there for dinner; he only wanted to listen. "Whoever that is," he mumbled, "they're pretty good."

When Mikey and Shalonda reached the end of the piece, a chorus of squeaky cheers went up. Both of them enjoyed the attention very much—almost as much as they had enjoyed making music together.

Chapter Twelve

In the morning, Shalonda woke up on the floor of Mikey's chamber and thought, *Isn't the sun out yet?* Then she smelled the damp earth and remembered where she was.

"Mikey," she whispered. "Are you here somewhere?"

"Huh?" Mikey answered. "Who? What?"

"It's me, Shalonda. You have to take me back above ground. I can't stay here—really—I have to go home."

Mikey thought she meant that her family would be worried, but she added, in a very small squeak, "I'm scared."

Although he was sad that she couldn't stay longer, he knew how it felt to be scared, and he said, "Hold on to my tail. I'll have you above ground in a minute or two."

And then they were off, trotting through tunnels, always going uphill. It was a bit awkward for Shalonda, hurrying along with Mikey's tail in one of her paws. She was glad he couldn't see her flopping from side to side.

The sunlight appeared up ahead as a gentle, dusty beam shining down through a small hole into the tunnel. Shalonda had never been happier to see light. Once they climbed up into the grass, though, she had to close her eyes because it was so painfully bright.

A robin sang a happy song, and Shalonda looked up into the maple tree, where she saw a little screech owl sitting upright on a branch. She had never seen an owl before, but something inside told her that the bird would eat them both in a blink if it caught them. "Mikey!" she whispered. "Let's get out of here!"

As they ran across the damp grass toward the house, she checked over her shoulder, and that's when she realized that the owl's eyes were closed. It was still sleeping!

If climbing down the three brick steps the night before had been hard, climbing *up* was twice as hard. Shalonda had to stand on Mikey's shoulders, and he had to rise up onto his tippy-toes. What made it even harder was that they were both slippery from running through the dew. It was a good thing that Shalonda was a slender little mouse.

Peeking through the crack under the door, she told Mikey, "It's safe. No cat in sight. Want to come in and look for cheese?"

Mikey hung his head. He didn't want to say good-bye to his friend, but he couldn't go back inside. His home was out here. "Sorry," he said.

Now Shalonda realized what Mikey already knew: that they wouldn't see each other again. She was a house mouse, and he was an underground dweller. Last night's duet would be their one and only concert.

"It was really nice meeting you," he told her.

"Come here, you goofy mole," she said and gave him a kiss on the cheek. When she was very, very close, he saw a tear about to fall from her eye.

A big lump grew inside Mikey's chest, something he had never felt there before. He had to leave fast before he started crying.

But first he had to get down those steps. *Plop! Plop! Plop!*

When Emma woke up, she was confused. She couldn't remember going to bed the night before—and why was she still wearing her clothes?

Seeing Susie beside her, she remembered Mikey. "Are you still in there, Mikey?" she asked.

He wasn't, and that worried her. Had something happened to him?

She ran around from room to room until she found her cat. "Open wide," she said and studied the cat's teeth. No sign of a recent meal there. But that didn't solve the mystery of where Mikey had gone.

Putting on her bunny slippers, she went down the front steps and circled the house, calling out to her little friend.

She went to the maple tree in the backyard and crouched down at the place where she had given Mikey his lessons. "Mikey, can you hear me? It's Emma. Please answer!"

There was no answer, and Emma began to cry, fearing that something terrible had happened to her friend because she'd fallen asleep.

"Why are you crying?" a tiny voice asked.

She wiped away the tears. There, poking up in the grass, was the little gray head of her friend, Mikey the mole.

He didn't understand why she scooped him up and stroked his back so many times with her finger, but he enjoyed the attention. "Are you okay?" he asked her.

She laughed. "Me? I was worried that you got eaten!"

He laughed with her. "Well, I almost did. But everything's okay now."

She lifted her hand to her face and pressed Mikey up against her cheek. From that scary height, he had a good view of her house, even if it looked like a blur to him. Somewhere inside was his friend Shalonda.

He wondered if he would ever see her again. And even though Emma kept stroking his fur, which felt wonderful, a heavy sadness came over him, unlike any emotion he had had ever known before.

Chapter Thirteen

"So, Mikey," Emma said, "now that you've seen an actual concert, what do you think? Would you like to perform on a stage like that?"

"I guess I would," he said. "But I don't see how it could ever really happen."

"Why not?"

"Well, for one thing, how would all those people even see me on that stage?"

Emma thought about that for a moment and solved the problem. "When rock stars give concerts in stadiums, they show big pictures of them on movie screens so the people far away can see. They could do that for you too."

"But my violin is so small—no one would be able to hear me."

"Yes, they would—because you'll have a microphone."

Mikey imagined himself on the same stage where the violinist had stood. It was a thrilling thought.

"Why don't you get your violin?" Emma said. "We have to start planning what you should play."

During their lesson, Mikey practiced on all the songs Emma had taught him. She was very proud of her little friend. For Mikey, though, something seemed missing. He was concentrating too hard on his playing to realize what it was, exactly . . . until he heard a familiar voice squeaking, "Mikey!"

He couldn't see her, but he could hear Shalonda scurrying through the grass toward him. He had never been so happy!

"What's the matter, Mikey?" Emma asked. "Why did you stop in the middle of the piece?"

"My friend is coming!" he said. "I didn't know if I'd ever see her again! Here she is!"

He set his violin down carefully, and then Shalonda rushed up to him and gave him such a big hug that she almost knocked him over.

Emma watched all this with a smile. Shalonda was not as amused. "Can you make her go away?" she whispered to Mikey.

"Why?" he asked. "She's my friend."

Shalonda shook her head and said, "I know, but she's a human. They don't like mice."

"I'll bet Emma likes mice," Mikey said and shouted up to her, "Hey, Emma! You like mice, don't you?"

It wasn't exactly the truth, but Emma said, "I think mice are just adorable, and I would really like to meet your friend."

Emma's words changed Shalonda's attitude completely. She decided that maybe not all humans were mean; this one, at least, seemed nice. "How do you do?" she said as politely as she could. "It's a pleasure to meet you."

"It sure is!" Emma said. "I've never met a mouse before, and I've never heard of one who could talk."

"Oh, we can all talk. It's just that most people don't bother to listen. They assume we can't do anything but steal cheese."

"I promise never to assume anything about mice again," Emma said.

"I'm so happy!" Mikey cried out. "I'm with my two best friends in the world!"

"Shalonda," Emma said, "would you mind if Mikey kept playing his violin? He wants to give a concert soon, and he needs to practice."

"I would *adore* listening to Mikey play," she said.

She had a little surprise waiting for Emma, but she kept that secret for now.

Mikey knew exactly what she was thinking. As he played "The Swan" from *Carnival of the Animals*, a very quiet voice joined in. The singer didn't sing words, just sounds that sometimes matched the violin's part and sometimes moved in lovely harmony. Emma's mouth hung open—just as Shalonda knew it would.

Around them, the flowers swayed as if moving to the lovely music. Mikey could hear worms wiggling up to the surface to listen, and he enjoyed the compliment. He even heard the old snake lift his head out of the grass to listen.

When the song ended, Emma applauded. "I never thought I'd hear anything like that!" she said.

"Little animals are full of surprises," Shalonda said.

While Emma tried to convince Shalonda to perform on stage with Mikey, the young mole sighed with happiness. He didn't really care whether or not he gave a concert someday. What thrilled him more than performing was knowing that he could come here every day and see both of his friends, Emma and Shalonda.

Together, they would make the most beautiful music.

The End

Index

Edwards Brothers Malloy
Oxnard, CA USA
November 26, 2014